A Curious George® Activity Book

I Am Curious About Reading

Featuring Margret and H. A. Rey's Curious George

SCHOLASTIC INC.

New York   Toronto   London   Auckland   Sydney

Activities by Frances Leos
Illustrations by Manny Campana

ISBN 0-590-41045-8

12 11 10 9 8 7 6 5 4 3 2   7 8 9/8 0 1 2/9

Printed in the U.S.A.   34

First Scholastic printing, September 1987

This is George.
He lives with the man
with the yellow hat.

George is a very curious monkey.
George is curious about you.
Write your name here.

_____

George is curious about your pets.
Draw a picture of your pet
or a pet you would like to have.

If you are curious
about the answers to the puzzles,
look in the back
of the book.

One morning, Curious George woke up early.
Put the pictures in the right order.

George looked out a window. Mr. Nelson
was walking his dog, Andy.
Draw a circle around the dog that is different.

George was curious. What would it be like to walk a pet?
Draw a circle around each animal that would make a good pet.
Draw an X over each animal that would not make a good pet.

Later that day, George rang Mr. Nelson's doorbell.
The shape of the doorbell is a circle.
Color the pictures below that have a circle shape.

The door was open. George went in.
Help George find Andy.

Andy looks like this: ➡

START

George found Andy inside the living room. The pictures below are some of the things George saw in Mr. Nelson's living room. Draw a circle around the things that feel hard. Underline the things that feel soft.

George also saw two of Mr. Nelson's other pets.

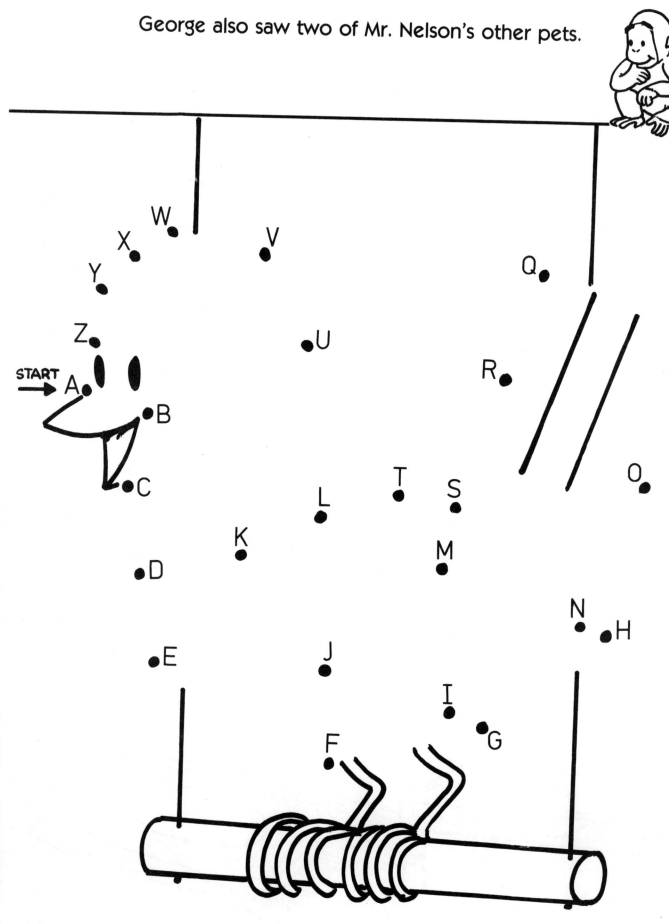

START → A

Connect the dots to see what they are.
The dots are in alphabetical order.

George tried to take all of the pets for a walk.
In each pair, draw a circle around the pet that is bigger.
Underline the one that is biggest of all.

In each pair below, draw a circle around
the animal that is smaller.
Underline the animal that is the smallest of all.

George tried to put a leash on the cat.
She ran away.
Color the pictures that rhyme with cat.

George opened the bird cage. The bird flew away.
Bird begins with the letter B.
Color the pictures that do not begin with a B.

What excitement! The pets all chased each other.
Mr. Nelson's alphabet soup spilled all over the floor.
Draw a line between the capital letters and the
small letters that go together.

Mr. Nelson came running in.
"What's going on here?" he shouted.
George was scared. He ran home.
Draw a line between each animal and its home.

George was still sure that the pets
wanted to go for a walk.
He went back to Mr. Nelson's house
with his wagon.
Color George brown.
Color his wagon red.
Color the wheels and the handles black.
Color the tree trunk brown.
Color the treetop green.
Color the fence blue.

George put the bird cage and the goldfish bowl into the wagon. Draw a circle around the two wagons that are exactly alike.

George tied the dog to the wagon.
Draw a circle around the picture that shows
the dog in front of the wagon.

The dog and George pulled the wagon.
The cat followed behind.
Look at the big picture.
Draw a circle around the little picture
that finishes the sentence.

  is behind the dog.

The dog is behind   .

George wanted to visit all the
pets in the neighborhood.
Every house with an A has a pet in it.
Help George visit all the pets.
Start from the top left-hand corner.

Mr. Jane's dog followed George and the pets.
But she left her puppies at home.
Draw a line between the animals and their babies.

Mary O'Brien's cat got in line behind the dog.
The line of pets got longer.
Draw a circle around the picture that
completes the pattern in each row below.

Every time George passed a house,
pets ran out and joined his line.
Look at the picture below.
Answer yes or no to the questions.

Do you see this? _____

Do you see this? _____

Do you see this? _____

Soon all the pets in the neighborhood
were following George.
It was a wonderful parade.
Draw a circle around the first pet in George's parade.
Draw a square around the last pet in George's parade.

George and the pets passed by a zoo.
George made up a poem.
Saying the pictures out loud
will help you read George's poem.

My pets and I
went walking two by two.
We said, "How do you do?"
to the animals at the zoo.

"Bow-wow," said my  .

"Oink-oink," said the

"Tweet-tweet," said my .

And the said, "Moo."

"Meow-meow," said my .

"Roar," said the

Three yelled, "Quack-quack-quack!"

And my stepped back.

My said, "Sqeek-squeek,"

to a furry .

Then we all said, " 'Bye! We'll come back very soon."

George and the pets stopped in front of a movie theater.
George's favorite movie was playing.
Use the code below to find out the title of the movie.
Say the word for each picture.
Put the first letter of the word
in the box below each picture.
When all the boxes are filled,
you can read the name of George's favorite movie.

The pets looked inside a balloon store.
Color the balloon that is different.

Everyone could see his shadow. Draw a line between each pet and his matching shadow.

George passed some girls jumping rope. They were chanting their ABC's as they jumped. Fill in the missing letters.

A _ C
_ _ H
_ _ N
E _ G
Q _ S
_ _ E
C _ L
J _ Q
O _ T
R _ W
U _ _
X _ Z

The food store was next to the clothing store.
Draw a circle around the things that
belong in a clothing store.
Underline the things that belong in a food store.

George loved all the toys in the toy shop window.
Draw a circle around the things that belong in a toy shop.
Draw something else that belongs in a toy shop.

George and the pets walked by a store that sold bows.
Color one bow with a color that begins with a Y.
Color two bows with a color that begins with a B.
Color three bows with a color that begins with an R.
Color four bows with a color that begins with a G.

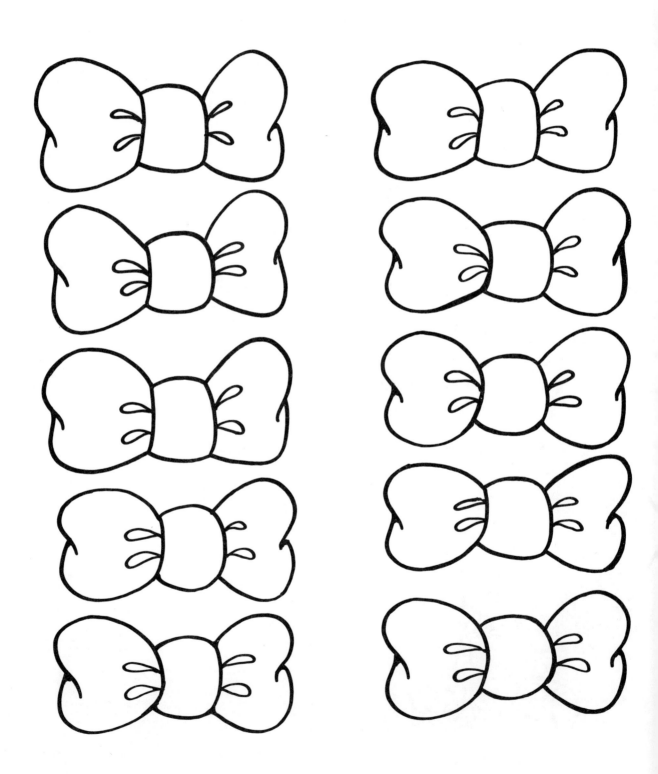

The wind was blowing kites high up into the sky.
There are five pairs of kites in the picture.
Draw a line between the matching pairs.

George's parade passed by a T-shirt shop.
The shirts in the window had many different patterns.
Copy the pattern of each T-shirt onto the one next to it.

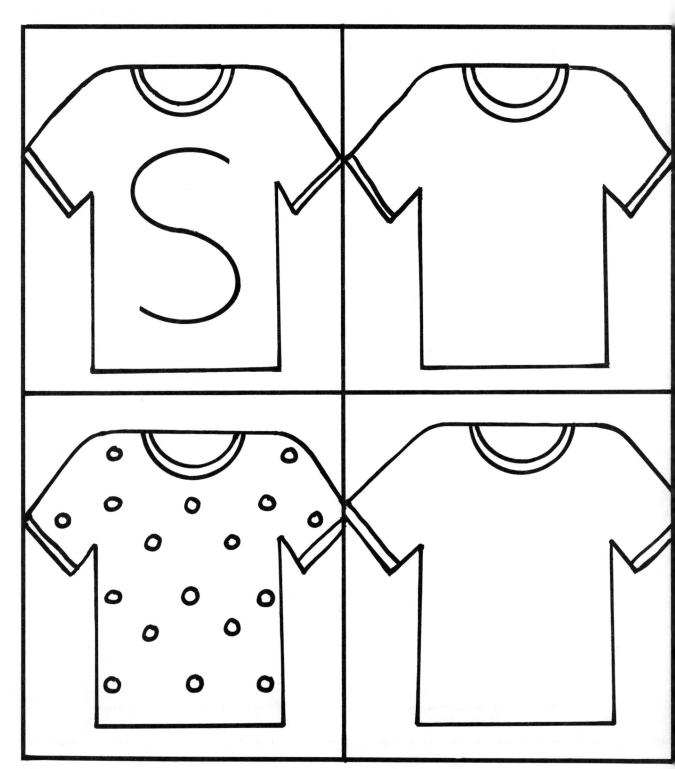

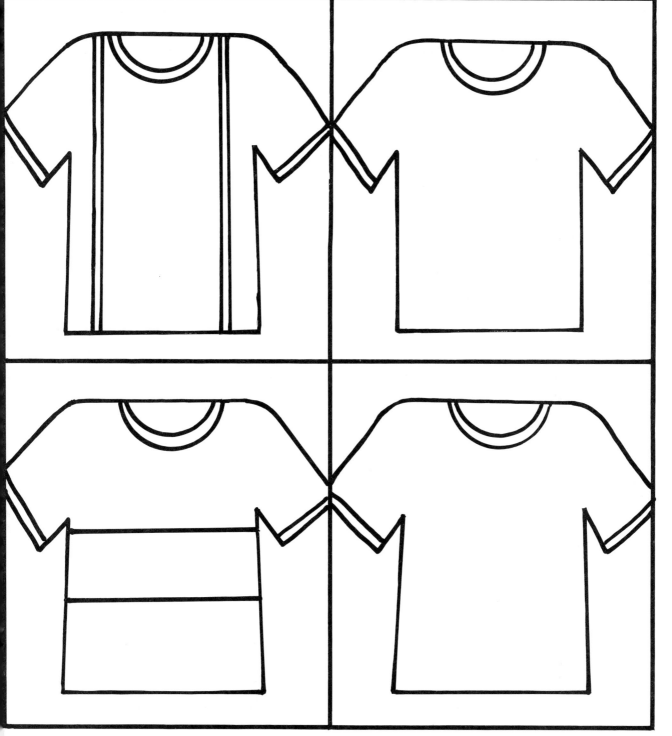

George and the pets walked by a park. They stopped to watch the children play. The middle picture is missing from the group below. Circle the small picture that goes with the big pictures above it.

Now do the same for this group.

George decided it was time to go home. All the pet owners were waiting at George's house. They were mad. These two pictures are not exactly alike.
Draw a circle around the things that are different.

George was scared.
George's name is written seven times in the picture.
Can you find all seven?

Mr. Jane said, "Wait! The pets look happy.
George is a good pet walker!"
"I could use a good pet walker," said Mary O'Brien.
Look at the picture closely.
Then take the memory test on the next page.

What did you see on page 43?
Draw a circle around the right picture in each row.

One by one, all the neighbors agreed
to let George walk the pets.
Look at the faces below.

Circle the faces that look happy.
Put an X on the faces that look angry.

Now everyone is happy. George will walk the pets every day. Draw a picture of something that makes you happy.

ANSWERS

Page 4. - The order is 4, 2
                              1, 3

Page 5.

Page 9.

Page 15.

Page 17.

Page 6.

Page 12.

Page 19.

Page 7.

Page 13.

Page 20.

Page 21.

Page 8.

Page 14.

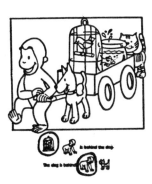

Page 23.

Page 33.

Page 39.

Page 24.

Pages 40 & 41.

Page 28.

George's favorite movie is BLUE BEAR.

Page 29.

Page 35.

Page 42.

Page 30.

Page 38.

Page 45.

Page 32.